The sun does arise,

And make happy the skies.

The merry bells ring

To welcome the spring

The skylark and thrush,

The birds of the bush.

Sing louder around,

While our sports shall be seen

On the echoing green

William Blake

James Has Diabetes

James

Story by Mariah Daly

Illustrations by Dawn Mahoney & Mariah Daly

AuthorHouse™
1663 Liberty Drive, Suite 200
Bloomington, IN 47403
www.authorhouse.com
Phone: 1-800-839-8640

First published by AuthorHouse   4/13/2009

ISBN: 978-1-4389-3188-3 (sc)

Printed in the United States of America
Bloomington, Indiana

This book is printed on acid-free paper.

authorHOUSE®

For: Ray, Cynthia, Katie, George, Marianne, Roanna, Gene, Sidney and Gwendolyn who listened and cared.

It is important for readers to understand that JAMES HAS DIABETES is a story about one boy's experience with Type 1 Diabetes. The message is meant to convey that Diabetes is a disease a child can live a healthy life with. It is not meant to prescribe, diagnose or treat. If you have questions or concerns contact your Doctor and Diabetic Educator.

Table of Contents

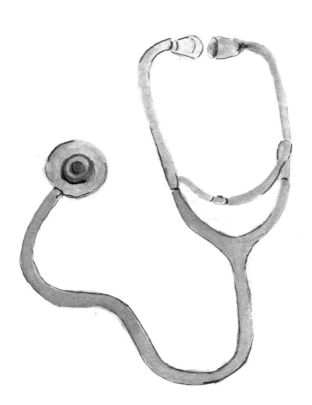

One

The Cove

Julia and James live in a New England town by the sea. They love running in the sand, throwing stones in the water, watching waves crash on the rocks, and gathering buckets of mussels. They like everything about their cove except the gray gloomy month of March that never seems to end.

The cove is made of sand, pebbles, rocks, cliffs and ocean. Tall sea grass grows in the sand. Seashells form intricate patterns on the beach. The ocean has its own majesty. The winds bring mussels entangled in seaweed to the shore, and high tides sweep them back to sea. All this beauty brings Julia and James many happy days.

The cove is located on the south side of town where there are many old houses. Julia and James live in a huge red Victorian house with eaves that protect them on windy days. In the winter birds find shelter in the eaves and in spring they build their nests. The town has a church, a hall, a school and an athletic field where Julia scores soccer goals and James hits home runs. Everyone in town knows that Julia and James can run like the wind.

Each season brings new adventures. In autumn Julia and James wave goodbye to their feathered friends flying south. Alvin the baker gives them both leftover breads to feed birds and ducks on cold winter days. In spring they watch parades of ducklings and loons learning to dive and fly. In summer they swim and build sandcastles. They love to sit on high rocks and sing.

This March was unusually dreary. Jeremiah the fisherman visited on rainy days. He told the children stories of famous sea captains whose ships crashed on rocks near their cove, leaving behind treasures buried at the bottom of the ocean.

Julia and James told Jeremiah, "When we grow up we'll learn scuba diving, find hidden treasures, and become rich."

"I'll build a baseball field," said James.

"I'll build a music school," said Julia.

Two

Not Feeling Well

On the very last day in March, James complained to Julia at breakfast. "This month has been so dreary. I don't like feeling tired and thirsty all the time. Yesterday I wanted to sleep all day."

Julia liked to share with her brother but watching him drink all of the orange juice each morning made her say, "James, save some orange juice for me. I need the energy for soccer practice."

James rarely yelled at his sister but his strong thirst made him reply, "I need the juice more than you do."

Every evening when homework was finished, Julia and James read or watched movies. On Wednesday evening a frown came over Julia's freckled face and it turned redder than her flaming hair.

Julia was not a sister who worried but this time she stood up, put her hands on her hips and said in a firm voice, "James I really like our time together, but it isn't much fun watching you snooze. After all, I could be reading or practicing the flute."

James was a boy who got mad at his sister's occasional impatience, but this time he didn't blink an eyelash. His dark brown hair and freckled face made him look paler than ever. He spoke to Julia in a quiet voice, "Enough of your noise, I don't feel well."

Mom said, "James this isn't like you. You are usually a bundle of energy."

The next day the sun was shining. It was the first day of April.

James blurted to Julia at the breakfast table, "Dreary March is over. Today's my first day of baseball practice."

When school bells rang in the afternoon James darted to the baseball field and waited in the dugout for his turn.

Brian the coach shouted, "James, you're up. We're counting on you. The bases are loaded."

James held the bat firmly in his hands and watched the ball like a hawk. His bat struck the ball and a loud cracking sound was heard throughout the field. When he reached second base he heard Julia yell from the bleachers, "Run James, run."

He felt groggy when he reached third base. His uniform was soaked with sweat. Cheers echoed throughout the field and everyone shouted.

He asked himself, "What's going on? I never felt this way before."

Brian the coach saw how exhausted James looked, so he walked him to the dugout and gave him a sports drink. James felt stronger after the sports drink, so he, and Julia and their friend Connor began walking home.

Connor stammered excitedly, "B-b-b-boy, oh boy, J-J-J-James, you are really great. I w-w-w-wish I could play as well as you."

"You can. Come to my house on Saturday and we'll practice. All you need to do is watch the pitcher, hold the bat firmly and look at the ball," replied James.

"That will be g-g-g-great," said Connor.

James and Julia didn't mind Connor's way of speaking because they liked him. They didn't like it when some of the kids made fun of him once in a while.

When James and Julia got home, James felt tired. He ate little for supper and went to bed early.

The sky was gray when James awoke. He sat down for breakfast but he was too groggy to finish his cereal. Mom looked at dad and you could tell that they were worried.

Finally mom spoke up. "We're going to visit Doctor O'Neill in her clinic."

"I want to go to," replied Julia.

Dad said, "Away we go."

James said, "I'll go only if we get home in time for baseball practice."

"A Nor'easter is predicted for today. Looks like practice will be cancelled." replied dad.

Three

To The Doctor

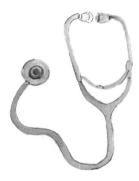

When they arrived at the clinic, buckets of sleet and hail poured from the sky, covering the ground with layers of ice. Julia fell on the sidewalk and bumped her knee. "Ouch," she cried, and then got up.

The nurse greeted them at the front desk. She led them down a long corridor with bright colors and into the examining room. James and Julia stood in the room and looked at shelves and counters filled with medical stuff, toys and children's books. The first counter held a big glass jar filled with cotton balls, and right next to it were a rubber hammer and a stethoscope. The next counter displayed needles with syringes and a jar with wooden sticks that looked like giant popsicle sticks. Many children's books lined the shelves.

The nurse asked, "James how is your appetite? Are you tired? Are you thirsty? Do you urinate more than you usually do?"

James replied, "How did you know this?"

She asked James to stand on the scale.

When mom looked at the scale record, she paused for a moment and said, "James, you've lost four pounds."

The nurse told him that she would draw a sample of blood from his arm and a drop of blood from his index finger. She explained to him how it would be done.

"Ouch," he mumbled, but before he knew it the stings went away.

In a few minutes Dr. O'Neill entered the room. Her face was kind and her voice firm. She asked the family to come into her office. When everyone was seated she spoke seriously with the family, and explained that James's blood sugar was high, and that this was the reason that James felt tired, thirsty, and sweaty. "When this happens in children James's age," she added, "a condition called Type 1 diabetes develops."

She took a diagram of the human body from her desk drawer and pointed to an organ and said, "This is called the pancreas. It is located right behind the stomach and it makes insulin to help the body metabolize sugar for energy. James's pancreas is not making enough insulin so we must treat this by giving insulin shots to him."

She told James that he would feel much better after he received the shot of insulin. Dr. O'Neill reached for a needle and syringe on the counter and explained that she would give him a shot in his arm. She wiped his arm with alcohol. After the needle pierced his arm, James looked Dr. O'Neill right in the face and hollered, "Two needles in one day are terrible."

The wind howled, causing the windows to shake. Dr. O'Neill looked out the window and said, "What a storm. I can barely see."

She continued, "When a child is diagnosed with diabetes he or she goes to the hospital that day." She paused and looked out the window and said, "Driving will not be safe and the nearest hospital is forty miles away."

James said to mom and dad in a firm voice, "I was in the hospital last year with bronchitis. You promised me that if I ever got sick again I could go to the hospital in the city."

Doctor O'Neill asked the family, "Do you know that Bryan the assistant coach is a Visiting Nurse? Does he live near you?"

"Yeah, two doors away. I didn't know he was a nurse," replied James.

Doctor O'Neill told the family that she would contact The Visiting Nurse Association and request that Bryan see them at home today: "There is a clinic in the city that treats people who have diabetes. The storm is supposed to end this evening. The roads will be plowed by morning. In the clinic you will be seen by a medical team. They'll teach and treat you as a family how to deal with diabetes in your life. Bryan will visit you today and tomorrow morning."

When the family arrived home and sat down for afternoon snack and decided to visit the clinic on the following morning after Bryan's visit.

Four

Bryan

After supper the family was watching the news. "Ring!" went the doorbell and in walked Bryan the nurse. James couldn't see his brown hair and freckled face, as a large hood covered his head, and for a moment James didn't recognize him. Everyone was happy to see him; James the happiest. After all he was the father of his friend Christopher and the assistant baseball coach too.

"I didn't know you were a nurse," said James.

"I wear many hats," said Bryan.

He opened up his backpack and took out some medical supplies with several baseball cards.

"What's that?" asked James as he pointed at a blue grey box.

"Glucometer," answered Bryan. "It sounds like this, glue-come-meter." Brian continued by explaining how blood sugar was checked with the glucometer.

"Connor and I can practice that word," thought James.

James put out his index finger while Bryan wiped it with an alcohol sponge. He barely felt the sting because seeing a drop of blood roll onto a thin piece of plastic fascinated him.

Everyone's eyes focused on the glucometer screen. All of a sudden the numbers 333 appeared. "It's a standup triple," shouted James.

"Similar but not quite," replied Bryan. "You see the normal target range of blood glucose is eighty to one hundred and twenty. A glucose check is taken just before meals and at bedtime. Now three, three, three is high because James just finished supper. Insulin is needed to help you break down sugar for energy, so that way you won't feel as tired after the shot."

Before you knew it Bryan took out two vials of insulin from his backpack and pointed to the first insulin bottle and said, "The first is clear fluid called regular insulin and it acts fast. The second is cloudy and is called N.P.H. insulin. It's longer acting and will take care of James all night. He'll need a light snack with the N.P.H. insulin right at bedtime." James couldn't believe his eyes as he watched Bryan draw up the insulin. Bryan's hand was so steady, and he didn't so much as blink an eyelash.

He told James, "We always draw up clear insulin first and then we add cloudy N.P.H." He explained what a shot would be like while he prepared. James barely felt the sting.

"Wow, Bryan, you're a pro at needles and baseball," exclaimed James.

"You're a pro at baseball and will be a pro at this one day." replied Bryan. He gave James several baseball cards and said, "I expect to see your picture on one of these real soon."

Mom walked Bryan to the door. She wanted to say thank you a hundred times, but there wasn't enough time so she thanked him just once.

Bryan replied, "Goodnight. See you in the morning."

James went to bed right after his bedtime snack. When he got under the covers, mom, Julia, and dad came into his room to say goodnight. He told them that he felt mad about missing baseball practice.   He said, "A lot happened today."

Mom said, "It's okay to be mad about missing baseball practice. We're very proud of you."

James said, "This was an awful day." He paused, "Except for Bryan."

Julia replied, "I'm with you all through this."

Dad tucked James under the covers and said, "You're great."

James fell fast asleep feeling the love of his family around him.

The next morning rays of sunlight streamed through James's windows. James awoke, darted into the shower, and then to the kitchen for breakfast.

Bryan was sitting at the kitchen table with dad, drinking coffee.

"Time for a glucose check and insulin," said Bryan.

"Not again!" grumbled James.

"Yes, again," replied Bryan.

The test and shot went by very fast and before you knew it James sat down for breakfast.

"My favorite," he exclaimed as he poured a second helping of whole grain cereal with fresh fruit into his cereal bowl.

Mom looked at Julia, and you could tell that they both were happy to see James's enthusiasm return.

Five

The City

The drive to the clinic was smooth since roads were plowed. When the clock struck four the family arrived at the hospital door, located on a busy city street. The hospital was many stories high. James counted thirty. He gazed up at this tall building.

Dad chuckled and said, "James, the roof of your mouth might get sunburned."

James replied, "Cool, it's more exciting than our little country hospital."

The receptionist gave them directions to the clinic for persons with diabetes. They walked down an infinite corridor and into a large office. The office manager brought them to the waiting room and they were introduced to the Medical Team. Cynthia, the nurse educator, said hello, as did Dr. Andrew, the pediatric diabetic doctor, and last but not least, Paula, the coordinator. Paula gave them a classroom schedule. Cynthia told them that James would stay in the hospital for a few days with a parent. Dad volunteered. Mom and Julia would stay at a nearby Bed and Breakfast. There would be classroom instructions every day.

James had to admit that it was awesome to have dad in the room. Dad reminded him of the time when they'd gone camping in Canada last summer and when they'd caught a giant bass and cooked it on the grill. James remembered the warmth of the campfire at night when he slept in his down sleeping bag. The memory was great. The very next moment James heard the sound of an ambulance outside his window. He saw doctors and nurses scurry up and down the corridor outside his room. He heard the cries, chatter, and laughter of other kids in the rooms next to his. He felt strange. He missed the loud cracking sound from his baseball bat when he hit home runs. He missed Connor, and the smells of fresh bread from Alvin the baker. He even missed Julia.

Dad said, "Let's go into the children's room."

When dad and James entered the children's room they saw Gennaro from the next room with his dad, Zaira from Africa was there with her mom and Ebony from Cambridge was there with her mom. A New Yorker David was there, too. He was tall with jet black curly hair. He told James that he had earned a black belt in karate this year.

The children sat down around a large table, and they played checkers and monopoly, until they were exhausted.

David said, "All I want is sleep."

When it came time for their bedtime insulin not an "ouch" was heard. They were too tired.

Six

The Classroom and New Friends

The next day was sunny. James and his family met in the front lobby of the hospital. When James looked at the waiting area he saw David and his own dad looking smart. He saw Zaira and her mom with wonderful African hats and robes on sitting close by. Ebony and her mom were dressed casually. He ran over to them.

Dad shouted, "Hey, James, we're in a hospital, not on a country road."

The families crossed the street together and entered a large brick building for their first classroom day. The room was unlike any other Julia and James had seen before.

James ran to one window and said, "C'mere Julia, there are offices out there."

Julia ran to the other window and said, "No, you come here. There are so many buildings outside. How could this be possible to see from one room?"

David couldn't stop laughing, and when he finally did he said, "You two are country kids. I live in New York and see this all the time."

Cynthia the nurse educator greeted them and asked everyone to sit around a large round table. She told them that there are just over two hundred thousand children in the United States with Type 1 diabetes. Thousands of these children visit this clinic every year. She continued by asking the children what they had learned about diabetes.

"The pancreas is located behind the stomach. It makes insulin to breakdown sugar for energy," recited Julia.

"My pancreas is not making enough insulin so I need help with insulin medicine," answered Zaira. She then blurted out, "What's the name, mom?"

"Injections, not shots," replied her mom.

David said he wanted to learn more about carbohydrates because he couldn't live without New York cheesecake. James told the class how wonderful Bryan was and how he drew up clear insulin first, then cloudy, just like a pro. Ebony said that she couldn't pronounce the word glucometer. She blurted, "Gluckometer."

"Just say (glue-come-meter) it's just that way." said James. "Glue-come-meter."

Cynthia continued with instructions, explaining to them that blood sugar could also be called glucose. Then she put four items on the table. The first was an alcohol sponge to clean your finger with; the second, a sharp to stick the side of your finger with; the third, a testing strip with a circle where your blood is to be placed; the fourth, the glucometer, that measures and records blood glucose.

James's dad put the glucometer in the palm of his hand. "It fits perfectly. This is mighty handy," he said.

"Seeing that it suits you so well, you can be our first volunteer," replied Cynthia. She explained the glucose check while demonstrating on James's dad.

"My turn now," he said gleefully.

James's dad practiced with Zaria's mom.

Although the children were eager to practice, they listened to Cynthia when she explained to them that they would learn when they were ready.

On the second day of instruction heavy rains were pouring down on the city streets. David lost his fire-engine red umbrella to the wind while crossing the street. Ebony's baseball cap blew far away and she couldn't get it because cars were coming.

David shouted," Don't worry, Ebony. I have a Yankees cap."

"Well, I'm from Boston and I want a Red Sox cap," replied Ebony.

Gennaro smiled and said, "Fenway Park isn't too far away. We can go there after class."

Everyone was happy to be in the classroom and watch the rain from indoors.

Cynthia stood at the head of the round table and put out several bottles of insulin. She asked everyone what he or she knew about insulin.

James told everyone that clear regular insulin is like a fast runner leaving first base. Julia said, "Cloudy N.P.H. insulin was like the fog that floats from the cove near their house and lasts for a long time." Ebony said that there were different kinds of insulin.

"Yeah," blurted Zaira. "My Doctor changed my insulin to Lantus last week. It's clear like spring water. It lasts for twenty four hours."

Cynthia told the children that Ebony had a good point. "There are different types of insulin. The type that works for you may change. We at the clinic and your doctor and diabetic educator at home will watch your glucose levels, guide your meal plan and monitor your insulin type and dose."

Cynthia asked for a volunteer while she demonstrated drawing up insulin with clear sterile water. David's dad volunteered. He and Cynthia worked as a team. At first he was a bit nervous, but before you knew it all the parents had practiced with each other.

Cynthia smiled and said, "You're almost as brave as your children."

Seven

Fun with Food

Brilliant rays of sunshine streamed through the windows on their third classroom day. Julia put on her sunglasses. Ebony covered her eyes. Zaira rested her head on the table.

David stood up and said, "We New Yorkers know what to do." He closed the blinds.

James stood up and said, "We country kids know what to do." He turned on the lights.

Everyone's eyes had adjusted to softer lighting and then Laurie, the dietitian, entered the room. She welcomed them while putting pamphlets and a few posters of fruits, vegetables, breads, meats, fish and poultry on the table.

Gennaro looked surprised and exclaimed, "Cool! These pictures look like our summer vegetable garden and the fruit trees in our orchard."

Laurie told them that today's talk would be about the everyday food we eat. She gave everyone a large sheet of paper with images of many different groups of food. Each food group had a large space under it for writing. She asked everyone to write in the food they ate on a daily basis under the appropriate group.

The children started writing immediately. Zaira wrote in the chicken first, vegetable second and the fruit category third. James and Julia started writing in the fish and poultry section. David looked for New York cheese cake and shouted, "Where's the deserts?"

Ebony filled up the page. Gennaro wrote in every group until his pen finally ran out of ink.

Zaira was so hungry that she stood up and said, "I can't help it, I've got to go to lunch right now."

"You won't have to go far. Lunch will be delivered in a few minutes," replied Laurie.

In exactly two minutes a man with rosy cheeks, a white uniform and chef's hat rolled in a cart with sizzling chicken, whole wheat bread, steaming vegetables and a dessert of sugar- free frozen yogurt that resembled a snow bank.

James couldn't believe his eyes. He gasped for breath and exclaimed, "Alvin the baker! What're you doing here?"

"Business is slow in the country. I work here once a week. My wife Gwendolyn and I stayed up all night preparing this feast," answered Alvin.

"And what are you doing here?" asked Alvin.

"Well, it's a long story. We'll talk later," answered James.

Laurie asked everyone to take medium portions of this delicious feast while Alvin spread their lunch on a long table in the back of the room.

Laurie spoke of the value of the foods they ate during lunch. Gennaro chose chicken, a salad, whole wheat bread and asparagus. Most of the other choices were similar.

"I'll continue to talk about this when I meet with you individually and we develop a meal plan similar to the one you already have," said Laurie.

"These are healthy choices," she continued. "Whole grain bread, that brown bread some of you may not like, gives you some nutrients that are in whole grain cereals and whole grain pasta. Yogurt is rich in calcium, and fresh and frozen vegetables have vitamins and minerals."

She asked everyone to take a break for an hour. It was special to be outdoors. Buds were sprouting, birds were singing, flowers were blooming and the air was filled with fragrance.

When they returned to class Laurie asked them to take out their pyramid exercise and said, "Let's talk about your present diet." Gennaro volunteered to share his daily foods with the group. He told them about the whole grain pasta, fresh fruits and vegetables, whole grain cereals, and yogurt that he ate on a daily basis.

David asked about New York cheese cake. Laurie told him he could eat a medium slice of cheese cake. Julia and James already ate fresh fish several times a week. Ebony and Zaira were proud of their vegetables, chicken, whole grain breads, and fresh fruits.

"Look how different our diets are," exclaimed David.

At this moment every one started to yawn. Laurie told them that this was a lot of new information. "It will take time to understand. I'll meet with each one of you tomorrow and we'll talk about your meal plan. These talks will continue when you come back for routine visits."

David closed his eyes and visualized New York cheese cake.

Julia snapped her fingers, saying to him, "Wake up! There are other desserts besides New York cheese cake."

Laurie told them they were the best class she had ever taught and then instructed them to find the last page in their information packet and look at the question section. Some of the questions were: Should I take a glucose tablet before I ride my bike for five miles? What should I do if I am at a party with too many sweets? If I am playing sports and I feel weak and sweaty, should I have my blood sugar tested or take a glucose tablet?

James answered, "I'd eat an apple before I go for a long bike ride. I'd take a glucose tablet with me."

Gennaro answered, "I'd eat an apple if I'm sweaty, take a glucose tablet, and go home for a blood glucose check."

Everyone participated, and they realized that there were several right answers to each question.

"It's almost five o'clock."

"Oh no," said Ebony "This is our last classroom day."

Julia looked at Zaira and they felt sad.

Gennaro said, "I'll eat apples from my orchard, and think of you guys."

When a tear rolled down Ebony's cheek, Laurie put her hand on Ebony's shoulder and said, "Now, now, it isn't that bad. There will be more classes like this. You'll visit us every month. All of you can arrange to visit on the same day."

Everyone exchanged e-mail addresses. Julia and James's mom invited all of them to a summer picnic at the cove near their home. When the clock struck five, church bells chimed and sang a song to the city to celebrate the end of a beautiful spring afternoon.

The next day, Friday was the last day of instruction, and it came too soon. Each child worked individually with Laurie as he or she developed a meal plan. Guess what? Their meal plans weren't too different from their present ones, just a bit more interesting.

In the afternoon David headed south-west to New York City. Julia and James headed north to their home by the ocean. Gennaro went east to plant a spring vegetable garden. Ebony and Zaira went west like two brave young pioneers.

Eight

Return to the Cove

It was dusk when mom, dad, Julia and James arrived home.

Dad sighed and said, "What a long day this has been."

Julia and James ran to Connor's house, and all three darted to their cove to sit on their favorite rocks and sing.

Julia and James were happy to be home. Sounds of crashing waves and foghorns were comforting to hear. Seeing their cove was wonderful. Julia said, "Can I touch the air? Can I pick up a stone?" James gathered up several stones. "Julia, watch me skip these stones on the water."

"Wow!" exclaimed Julia as stones flew like rockets through the air and made circles as they slapped one ocean spot and then another.

Jeremiah, the fisherman who was in his boat just off shore heard the children.

"Welcome home," he shouted. His voice was so happy that the waves would have danced if they could. He rowed his boat to shore, put his daily catches in a sack and walked over rocks and sand to greet the children.

In the meantime mom and dad sat in the kitchen planning supper.

Mom sighed, "I can't look at another list."

Just then, Jeremiah entered the kitchen, took two fresh mackerels out of his sack and said, "Why not steam up vegetables and prepare a salad. I'll make the fish."

Julia, James and Connor darted off to Alvin the baker to fetch deserts. Every piece of pastry looked wonderful. The decision was difficult, but after some time they decided to buy six sugar-free blueberry muffins.

At supper, it was agreed that dad and James would be in charge of glucose checks and insulin. Julia and mom would be in charge of the planning and preparation of healthy meals. They would switch in May.

"Yeah!" shouted Julia and James. "Dad can really cook."

James and Connor made a spot in the family room for glucose checks and insulin. They put a poster of David Ortiz on the wall and hung up several baseball caps, while mom and Julia made a book to record blood glucose levels and insulin dosages.

Endless hours of catch-up homework filled the weekend hours. James refused to rewrite his composition again. Julia stamped her feet, saying, "I'll never do another decimal problem."

"Monday already!" shouted dad as music from the radio sang a wake-up call. James darted into the shower, and before you knew it he and Dad were in the family room checking the glucometer record. It read 100. James watched dad pierce the needle into his arm. Not an "ouch" was heard. Stings go away and James was now fully convinced that one day he would become a famous baseball player.

Julia and James put on their jackets and grabbed their lunch. Just as James was about to dash out the door, dad told him to see the school nurse before lunch for a glucose check.

"The principal called yesterday, and everyone is looking forward to your return," said dad.

Nine

Return to School

The walk to school was challenging, because Julia and James had become spoiled by city life. They separated and went to their classrooms.

The teacher, Ms. Alicia, greeted James at the door. "I spoke with your father and he told me about your week in the city," she said.

Upon entering his classroom James saw all kinds of signs welcoming him all over the walls. Feeling happy, he said to his classmates, "You're great! It's nice to be back."

Morning class flew by and before you knew it bells rang for lunch. Children darted to the cafeteria and James headed to the school nurse's office. His blood glucose read 102.

"In range," said nurse Debra.

James told Debra that he wouldn't need insulin with this reading, since his blood sugar was in a good target range.

"My readings have been in this range for a week. My family and I keep a close watch on the numbers. We learned a lot about diet, exercise and insulin at the clinic. We're still learning."

Debra replied, "Oh! Well, so am I."

He told Debra about the lunch Julia and mom prepared. A cheese and tomato sandwich on whole wheat bread, low-fat yogurt, an orange and a small bag of low-fat wheat crackers. Debra looked amazed and said, "I'm impressed."

James hurried to the cafeteria and looked for his classmates. When he saw them, he dashed to their table. Not a chair was empty. All were silent. Even Christopher, who never had a quiet moment in his waking hours, was still. Garrett turned his head away. James felt awkward and walked to the far end of the cafeteria and sat down at an empty table. He opened his lunch, bit into his cheese sandwich, and felt like the cheese in the Farmer in the Dell when the cheese stood alone. While he was eating his sandwich an upper class student sat down next to him and asked him if he was the boy she had just seen in the nurse's office. She told him that her name was Kate.

"I'm there every day to have my blood glucose checked," said Kate.

"So there's another kid in the school who has diabetes," replied James.

"Yeah, there are five of us. We meet once a week. Alvin the baker is our advisor." replied Kate.

"Alvin the baker! How did he get into this? He's everywhere. He was at the clinic and prepared a delicious lunch for us."

Kate told him that Alvin had developed Type 2 diabetes several years ago and that since then Alvin and his wife Gwendolyn had devoted lots of time to preparing fun, healthy food.

"They started an adult club and a children's club. We've been invited to a few of the adult meetings. Lots of fun, and we have great healthy desserts."

Kate told James to eat with his classmates, as it was a rule of their club to do so. "We can share our healthy foods with them," said Kate

"They won't eat with me," sighed James.

"That'll change." said Kate with a big smile on her face.

"When?" shouted James.

"Soon," replied Kate.

Bells rang, telling students to return to class. The children walked slowly, laughing and chatting. When Kate and James parted, James walked alone to his classroom. Upon entering the classroom he saw chairs arranged in a circle.

"It's talk time," shouted several students.

Ms. Alicia began the discussion and said, "Last week we talked about James's absence. He had an interesting week at a diabetes clinic in the city with his family. He learned a lot about diabetes, and we will too."

Suddenly the room became still. A pin drop would have sounded like thunder.

James blurted, "I missed you guys at the cafeteria."

"It's g-g-g-great to have you back," muttered Connor.

Garrett said, "I'm sorry about the cafeteria. You really should eat with us every day."

James replied, "I plan to, and I'll share my healthy lunches with you."

"I thought I'd catch diabetes from you," blurted Briana.

William whispered, "I didn't know what to say."

"Can I help?" asked Marianne.

Ms. Alicia suggested that she could bring fresh fruit to the dugout. Christopher offered to bring fruit also.

Ms. Alicia had a book about juvenile diabetes and shared the story with the students. James told them about the clinic and his new friends. He also talked about fun, healthy foods.

Bells rang to celebrate the end of a school day. Children dashed to their lockers and headed in different directions.

Connor, Christopher, Marianne and James walked together. James told them about his adventures in the city.

They shouted, "Awesome."

Marianne said, "We're going to the Science Museum next year."

When James arrived home he went into the kitchen for a snack, and before you knew it dad was checking his blood sugar. It read 200. Dad looked puzzled. James rolled his shirtsleeve up and pretended to be brave. Dad didn't utter a word. James's face turned bright red and he blurted. "I ate a brownie." Dad suggested that he eat an apple and half a brownie for tomorrow's snack.

Meanwhile Julia came home after soccer practice exhausted and in tears. "My team lost. I'm famished."

She helped herself to a large piece of cake.

Shortly afterward, when supper was served, James picked at his food and Julia helped herself to his leftovers.

Feeling sad, he went to his room to finish his homework and grumbled to himself, "Julia doesn't have her blood checked four times a day. She doesn't have to take insulin shots. Why me?"

James was quiet during his glucose check and insulin shot.

Shortly afterward, Julia came to his room to say goodnight and told her brother about her disappointing soccer defeats.

"Why can't I play as well as you?" asked Julia.

"I think you're a terrific player, Julia. Don't let one defeat get you down. Let's get a good night sleep so we can play tomorrow."

James couldn't fall asleep because he kept thinking of the times when he'd eat two brownies after baseball practice. Although he knew that his new meal plan was healthy, he still wanted to eat brownies and ice cream like everyone else. He remembered the classroom in the city where Laurie had spoken about "balancing," as she told the class that they could eat a small candy bar in place of an apple. She'd given them a booklet about this. He remembered Gennaro's stories about his apple orchard. He was beginning to like apples.

He thought to himself, "I'll read the pamphlet and talk to mom and dad tomorrow. We can look at Laurie's handouts and come up with new ideas. Maybe I can have a small scoop of ice cream with a half an apple." It didn't take long for James to fall fast asleep.

The following morning a thick fog floated over the ocean like a puffy grey blanket.

"It better clear up. We have a baseball game today." said James. His wish came true as beams of sunlight chased the fog away.

Ten

Victory

James was not the kind of boy who spent a lot of time observing the beauty of nature, but this time he gazed at the baseball field and said to Connor, "This is the most beautiful baseball diamond in America."

"It will b-b-b- bring us victory," replied Connor.

April showers had turned the baseball field grass into a brilliant green. A soft breeze cooled the dugout as the sun cast light throughout the field. "Connor, you're up before me. You can do it," said James.

"I'll d-d-d-do my b-b-b-best, replied Connor.

James watched Connor when he stood in the batter's box and saw a look of determination on his face that he had never seen before.

"Strike one," hollered the umpire, forcing Connor to look more determined.

Connor focused on the pitcher's throw. When his bat struck the ball a cracking sound like a thunderbolt was heard throughout the field. Connor dashed like a deer to first base, with Christopher on second and Garrett on third.

The team's enthusiasm was at an all time high. In the past James's standup triples and grand slams had pulled the team through many hard times. James felt nervous as he went to bat. It was the end of the ninth inning. He hadn't practiced in a week, bases were loaded.

He muttered to himself, "I can do it. Diabetes hasn't changed me."

When he swung the bat and hit the ball, the loudest crack sound ever to be heard echoed through the field. The ball flew into the air like a rocket and was never found again.

While James was running the bases he imagined himself in ten years making standup triples in Fenway Park with Jon Lester pitching. "I can see it now," thought James. "Julia, Connor, Garrett, David, Gennaro, Ebony and Zaira will be in the bleacher cheering me on."

James felt weak and sweaty when he reached the dugout as the team cheered. Bryan's face had the biggest smile James had ever seen. Bryan had made a baseball card with James's picture on it, and he gave the card to James before he checked his glucose.   It read 70. Feeling disappointed, James took a glucose tablet and shared an orange with Marianne.

The game was over as James's grand slam brought victory. The team hopped on their bikes and asked James to join them as they were heading to Bobby's ice cream stand.

James said, "Not today."

Connor and James began their journey home.

"I'm proud of you." exclaimed James.

"I'm p-p-p-proud of you." replied Connor.

James said, "I love the way you clocked it Connor. Right on the sweet spot!"

James

Connor replied, "Y-y-y-yeah. It was our h-h-h-hits that w-w-w-won it."

James grinned.

They continued walking and suddenly James put his head down and grumbled, "I've got to go home for a glucose check."

"I've g-g-g-got to go to my s-s-s-speech therapist. She h-h-h-helps me. I p-p-p-practice an hour every day. It's h-h-h-hard for me too. I w-w-w-wish I could be eating ice c-c-c-cream too," blurted Connor.

"Connor, I have a fun word for you. It's glue-come-meter. It's the little blue grey box that records my glucose check. We'll practice it tomorrow," said James with a big smile on his face. James and Connor parted and James continued on his journey home.

Eleven

Why Me

Walking by himself, James shouted, "Boy, oh boy! Look at me, a champion of grand slams. My picture is on a baseball card. Where's the team? Riding their bikes to fetch ice cream? What did I do? I shared fruit with Marianne. A bike ride could bring my glucose down. Now I need to go home for my glucose check."

Dusk began. The air was silent. Although James was tall for his age the long shadows that cast themselves on his path made him look a foot taller. He laughed to himself, "I'm getting taller by the minute." But he picked up a large stone and shouted, "Why me?"

Just as he was about to throw the stone at a wooden fence, James heard a loud voice coming from the firehouse at the end of the path.

"James, come on over and join us."

He looked across the street and you will never guess who it was: Lieutenant Donald and Leo the firefighter. Donald congratulated James on his grand slam and told him that it had been announced on the local news.

"We're real proud of you," said the two fire fighters, and they shook his hand.

Twelve

A Magnificent Supper

Donald, James, and Leo stood in front of the firehouse for some time and James said, "The game was awesome. Connor got his first hit."

Donald was quiet for a few moments, and then he asked James to join him for supper at Alvin's.

"Alvin the Baker! Not him again. He should be mayor!" exclaimed James.

"I just wanted to invite you to the bakery for supper, as I'm a Type 2 diabetic and our club meets tonight," answered Donald

"I can't go. I've got to go home for a glucose check and supper," replied James.

"You can call home from Alvin's and we'll take care of the glucose check and insulin at the bakery. Alvin has a glucometer and insulin. He can get instructions from your family about treatment." said Donald.

"Okay," replied James gleefully. "Sounds like a plan."

Upon arrival at the bakery Alvin greeted them with gusto. Donald called James's family for instructions.

James saw Gwendolyn's beautiful table setting. The plates and water glasses looked like illustrations that James remembered seeing in English fairy tales. He couldn't wait to eat, but the blood glucose check came first. It read 98.

"Bravo, in target range," cheered Donald. Then he checked his own blood glucose.

Alvin and Gwendolyn put a sign in the window that said: BAKERY CLOSED. FOR DIABETICS ONLY. Jeremiah the fisherman was turned away.

Everyone bowed their head to say grace. The meal was delicious: skinless broiled chicken with spinach, low-fat cheese and mushrooms over whole grain pasta, not to mention string beans and a large salad.

"This is more fun than a birthday party!" exclaimed James, who felt comfortable with these friendly adults. In fact he felt so comfortable that he asked them if he could try on their hats. The chef's cap and fireman's helmet were a bit large, but in a curious way they suited him.

James looked puzzled and blurted out, "I thought I was going to be a famous baseball player when I grew up, but look, these hats fit."

Donald looked at James and said, "James, you're going to have many choices in life. You can be whatever you want to be."

When Gwendolyn served a dessert of fresh fruit and sugar free frozen yogurt, James exclaimed, "This is the best supper of my life!"

During dessert everyone talked about his experience with diabetes.

"Why did this happen to me?" asked James.

Donald and Alvin told James that they had felt the same way he did when it was discovered that they had diabetes. Yet they both said that living with diabetes becomes easier with time.

"Besides there's ongoing research every day with new breakthroughs occurring in the treatment of diabetes. I read in The Diabetic Newsletter last week that a sensor has been developed and it can measure blood glucose twenty four hours a day. It's being tested and it might be available to us in a few months, said Donald.

"Cool," replied James.

Alvin told James that his Doctor had recently prescribed an insulin pump for him. "I'll see him in the city tomorrow and Cynthia will give me instructions."

 "Why can't I have one of those pumps?" asked James.

"You will, when your Doctor thinks you're ready. When the time comes Cynthia will teach you about the pump. The medical team watches us carefully. My doctor told me I'd need insulin shots for some time, but he thinks that I'm ready to adjust to the insulin pump," replied Alvin.

Thirteen

A New Chapter

James and Donald thanked Alvin and Gwendolyn for a wonderful evening and started on their journey home. Fog horns echoed throughout the town as seagulls covered the sky with a black night blanket. The stars and moon cast a soft light upon their path.

When James arrived home he shook Donald's hand like a proud grown-up and then ran upstairs to his room. For a moment he felt so tall that he thought his head would hit the ceiling.

He shouted, "Boy, oh boy, am I special! I made a grand slam and brought our team to victory. My picture is on a baseball card. Maybe I can rest up after the next game and get on my bike and join the team at Bobby's ice cream stand. I'll eat sugar-free frozen yogurt. I'll read the pamphlet Laurie gave us on substitutes and talk to mom and Julia about a small scoop of ice cream. I had supper with the most important adults in town."

Dad was in the living room when James arrived home. He followed him up the stairs to his room and checked his glucose. It read 100.

"Hurrah," cheered James. "In target range."

As dad was preparing James's cloudy N.P.H. insulin, a dense fog floated in from the ocean and settled around their home and over the landscape. Moisture from the fog nourished trees, shrubs and plants throughout the night. The cloudy NPH insulin nourished James as it converted sugar into energy. A peaceful expression settled on James's face as he thought of this wonderful day and of the happy days to come.

About the Author

Mariah Daly was educated at Laboure College for a Nursing degree, Harvard Extension with Radcliffe Institute for a Bachelors Degree in The Humanities and Lesley University for a Masters Degree in Education. She has published papers in Nursing Journals and has written policy and protocol about patient and nursing education in hospitals. She studied watercolor and pottery with several Boston artists. She won blue and red ribbons in The Annual Beacon Hill Art Walk for her works of art. She currently practices nursing in Boston and has taught children in afterschool programs in Boston and Cambridge. Mariah is a member of Diabetic Educator's of Western Mass. She is a member of The Board of The West End Branch and The Friends of The West End Branch of The Boston Public Library where she is involved with community and program development. JAMES HAS DIABETES is her first book.

Dawn Mahoney studied in Boston at The Museum of Fine Arts in a special program. She has also studied with artists in Boston, Montreal and Quebec. Her permanent art works are displayed in The Winthrop Town Hall, across the United States, France, Australia and Canada. She won a silver medal at New England's Spring Flower Show in Boston for a collective artistic mural. Dawn's current artistic involvements include President of The Winthrop Art Association, teaching and full time painting. She lives in Winthrop with her mother, sister and two grandchildren.

Printed in the United States
147576LV00002B